GUMBALL'S ~~FIRST~~ DANCE
Last

BY ERIC LUPER

CARTOON
NETWORK
B O O K S

AN IMPRINT OF PENGUIN RANDOM HOUSE

THERE IS A PENGUIN HIDING SOMEWHERE ON THIS PAGE. I HAVE CREATED A SERIES OF CHALLENGES, EACH MORE DANGEROUS AND PUZZLING THAN THE LAST, TO LEAD YOU—

IT'S RIGHT THERE IN THE MIDDLE OF THE PAGE, GUMBALL.

UGH! YOU RUINED IT!

CARTOON NETWORK BOOKS
Penguin Young Readers Group
An Imprint of Penguin Random House LLC

Photo credits: background images used throughout interior: (rice paper) © Thinkstock/rusm, (notepad paper) © Thinkstock/koosen, (Japanese paper) © Thinkstock/morningarage, (torn paper) © Thinkstock/kay, (white background) © Thinkstock/scyther5, (crumpled paper) © Thinkstock/koosen, (hardwood floor) © Thinkstock/mihalis_a, (pink paper) © Thinkstock/AKIsPalette; page 79: (scissor icon) © Thinkstock/tkacchuk.

Published in 2015 by Cartoon Network Books, an imprint of Penguin Random House LLC, 345 Hudson Street, New York, New York 10014. Printed in the USA.

ISBN 978-0-8431-8312-2

10 9 8 7 6 5 4 3 2 1

NUGGA-NUGGA.

MEEP.

SPRINGA-WINGA.

OKAAAAAY . . .
I'VE GOTTA GO.

WHAT'S THE USE OF GOING TO THE DANCE WITH PENNY IF I CAN'T EVEN TALK TO HER?
THAT'S NOTHING A FEW YEARS OF SPEECH THERAPY WON'T CURE!
DON'T WORRY, GUMBALL. WE'RE JUST GETTING STARTED.

SUSSIE'S PARENTS

LET'S CUT TO THE CHASE, GUMBALL. I'LL GIVE YOU A THOUSAND DOLLARS TO ASK SUSSIE TO THE DANCE. IT WOULD MAKE SUSSIE VERY HAPPY.

I'M NOT SURE SUSSIE IS EVER *UN*HAPPY.

LOOK, SUN! LOOK, BALL! LOOK, DOG!

AND I'M NOT SURE SUSSIE'S PARENTS ARE A VERY GOOD EXAMPLE OF A GREAT COUPLE.

THESE COUPLES ARE ALL A LITTLE CRAZY.

AND A LITTLE GROSS.

SOMEHOW, I KNEW YOU'D SAY THAT. SO, I TOOK IT UPON MYSELF TO DO A LITTLE RESEARCH.

WHAT SORT OF RESEARCH?

I CALL IT . . .

SO, WHAT WERE THE RESULTS, ANAIS?

THEY WERE SORT OF ALL OVER THE PLACE.

WHAT DO YOU MEAN?

LET'S HAVE A LOOK . . .

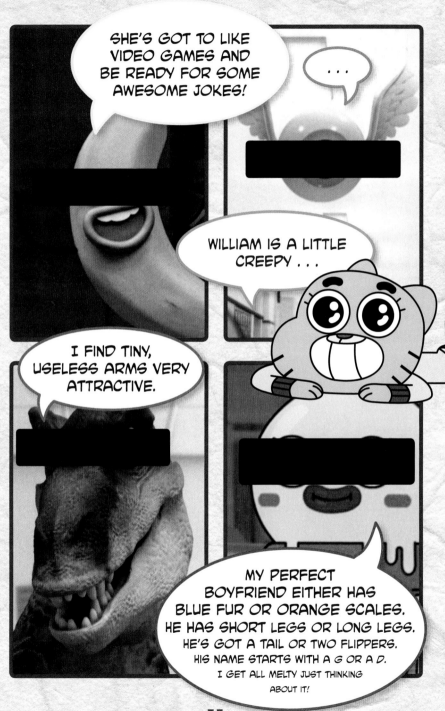

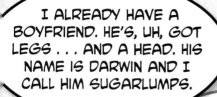

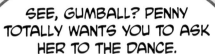

WE'RE GOING TO PLAY A LITTLE GAME CALLED M.A.S.H. IT'S GOING TO HELP YOU FIGURE OUT YOUR ROMANTIC FUTURE.

HOW'S IT GOING TO DO THAT?

JUST LISTEN TO HER, GUMBALL. SHE'S ONLY FOUR AND SHE'S IN JUNIOR HIGH. ANAIS IS SMARTER THAN BOTH OF US PUT TOGETHER.

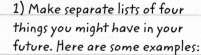

RULES

1) Make separate lists of four things you might have in your future. Here are some examples:

- ○ Mansion, Apartment, Shack, House
- ○ 1, 2, 3, 4 children
- ○ Any four kids in your class as a spouse
- ○ Four different types of transportation
- ○ Four different types of pets
- ○ Four jobs, etc. . . .

(Make sure some of them are awesome, but some are funny)

2) Pick a random number from the grid below by closing your eyes, spinning the book, and pointing.

5   8   4

6   2   7

9   1   3

3) Count down your different lists, crossing off the item that comes up on whatever number you've randomly chosen.

4) Continue counting around the circle until you have one item left in each list. Circle those items.

5) Tell your story!

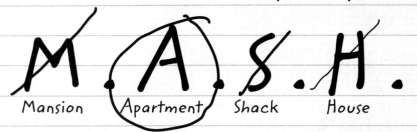

M. A. S. H.
Mansion   Apartment   Shack   House

CHILDREN	SPOUSE	TRANSPORTATION
~~1~~	~~Masami~~	~~Scooter~~
~~2~~	~~Teri~~	~~Parasail~~
(3)	(Penny)	(Pogo Stick)
~~4~~	~~Tina Rex~~	~~Ferrari~~

SEE, GUMBALL? THE M.A.S.H. BOARD SAYS YOU'LL BE MARRIED TO PENNY, LIVE IN AN APARTMENT, GET AROUND ON A POGO STICK, AND HAVE THREE CHILDREN.

I HOPE I DON'T LIVE DOWNSTAIRS FROM YOU WITH ALL THAT POGO-STICKING GOING ON IN YOUR APARTMENT.

M.A.S.H.

Mansion   Apartment   Shack   House

5   8   4   <u>BEST FRIEND</u>

6   2   7

9   1   3

_____

_____

_____

_____

<u>PET</u>   <u>JOB</u>

_____   _____

_____   _____

_____   _____

_____   _____

M.A.S.H.

Mansion   Apartment   Shack   House

5 8 4
6 2 7
9 1 3

FAVORITE FOOD

_____
_____
_____
_____

COLLEGE

_____
_____
_____
_____

FUN SPORT

_____
_____
_____
_____

Come up with as many categories as you like
and entertain your friends!

SO, IF THE M.A.S.H. BOARD IS RIGHT, PENNY AND I ARE GOING TO END UP TOGETHER.

THE M.A.S.H. BOARD NEVER LIES, GUMBALL.

SO, THAT MEANS I DON'T HAVE TO ASK HER TO THE DANCE. DESTINY WILL SOMEHOW TAKE OVER.

SILENT FURY

SILENT FURY

NO, SILENT FURY LOOKS LIKE THIS.
SHE'S GIVING YOU *I KNOW YOU LET ME DOWN.*

GUMBALL, WHAT ARE YOU DOING?

WHAT'S IT LOOK LIKE? WE'RE PLAYING VIDEO GAMES.

HOW WILL PLAYING VIDEO GAMES HELP YOU GET PENNY TO GO TO THE DANCE WITH YOU?

IT WON'T, BUT IT'S A LOT EASIER THAN TALKING TO A GIRL.

DEAR PENNY,
WOULD, YOU
LIKE TO GO
OUT TO THE
DANce WITH
ME? if yOU
dON'T, i WOULD
BE veRy Sad.
fROM,
Gumball

MOST OF A PERSON'S FIRST IMPRESSION OF SOMEONE COMES FROM BODY LANGUAGE AND SELF-PRESENTATION.

THAT SETTLES IT, ANAIS. I'LL GET DRESSED UP, PUT ON MY SWAGGER, AND MARCH RIGHT OVER TO PENNY'S HOUSE. SHE'LL BE SO IMPRESSED THAT *SHE'LL* ASK *ME* TO THE DANCE.

WHY DIDN'T I THINK OF THIS SOONER?

WHAT'S THAT, ANAIS?

WE NEED TO STUDY MR. AND MRS. FITZGERALD. IF THERE'S ANYONE PENNY WILL MODEL HER FUTURE RELATIONSHIPS AFTER, IT'S HER OWN PARENTS!

THAT SETTLES IT. I'M GOING TO ASK PENNY TO GO TO THE DANCE WITH ME. IT'S JUST LIKE TALKING TO ANYONE, RIGHT?

GO FOR IT, GUMBALL!

Budda-gudda = Hi there, Penny.

Dinga-donga = I am curious to know . . .

E. pluribus unum = Out of many, one.

Meep-murp = if you would like to go

Hunga-munga = to the dance with me

Rick-rock-rook = on Friday night.

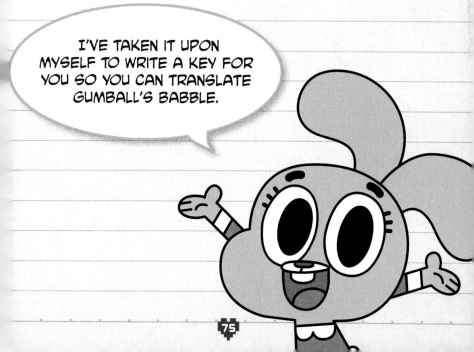

I'VE TAKEN IT UPON MYSELF TO WRITE A KEY FOR YOU SO YOU CAN TRANSLATE GUMBALL'S BABBLE.

REMIND ME WHY I MADE SUCH A BIG DEAL ABOUT ASKING PENNY TO THE DANCE . . . ?

Make Your Own Cootie Catcher

. Using scissors, cut out the cootie catcher along the lines indicated.

. Fold two opposite diagonal corners together, then open back up.

. Fold the other two opposite diagonal corners together, then open back up.

4. With the printed side down, fold all four corners into the center.

5. Flip over so the Gumball characters are facedown.

6. Again, fold all four corners to the center.

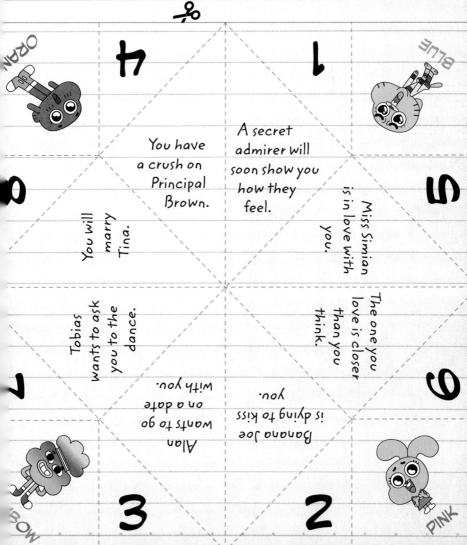

7. Fold any two sides together. Make sure the numbers are on the inside, and the characters are on the outside.

8. Slide your thumbs and index fingers under the four flaps.

9. Finally, pinch your thumbs and index fingers together. Your coot catcher is ready to go!